Anonymous

Industrial Monograph

on the pottery and classware of the central provinces

Anonymous

Industrial Monograph
on the pottery and classware of the central provinces

ISBN/EAN: 9783337386993

Printed in Europe, USA, Canada, Australia, Japan

Cover: Foto ©Andreas Hilbeck / pixelio.de

More available books at **www.hansebooks.com**

INDUSTRIAL MONOGRAPH

ON THE

POTTERY AND GLASSWARE

OF THE

CENTRAL PROVINCES,

for the Year 1895.

Published by Authority.

Bombay:

PRINTED AT THE

EDUCATION SOCIETY'S STEAM PRESS, BYCULLA.

1895.

INDUSTRIAL MONOGRAPH ON THE POTTERY AND GLASSWARE OF THE CENTRAL PROVINCES

FOR THE YEAR 1895.

POTTERY AND GLASSWARE

OF THE

CENTRAL PROVINCES.

The manufacture of pottery in these provinces has never risen to the level of an art. Only the simplest articles, and those, too, of the rudest workmanship are produced. It would be unfair to attribute this to an absolute want of artistic preception, for the vessels in ordinary use, though simple in design, are usually true in their proportions and graceful in outline, but the ease with which the raw materials is everywhere obtainable and the simplicity of the methods of manufacture have rendered articles of pottery so cheap that no importance is attached to their preservation. Hindus believe that an earthen vessel once used is tainted, and on certain occasions, such as the occurrence of a death in the family, the whole stock of earthenware is destroyed. It is consequently not worth while for the potter to spend much time or trouble on the ornamentation of his ware.

The Kumhár caste has the monopoly of the manufacture of pottery. Caste All castes, even Brahmans, will at times make their own bricks and tiles, and in some districts this industry seems to have fallen entirely into the hands of other castes as in Bhandára, where the Mahárs are said to have completely ousted the Kumhárs from this branch of their trade. In Seoni, too, the Kumhárs are said to think it beneath their dignity to make bricks, and this work is done by the Mehra caste. But pottery proper is manufactured solely by the Kumhár caste.

The caste is said to owe its origin to the illicit union of Brahmans with certain of the Kshatria tribes, but there is also a legend that on the occasion of his marriage with Sati, Siva created a man and a woman from the beads of his necklace and bade them set to and make pots for the ceremony. In Sambalpur, where the name retains the earlier form of Kumhár, the caste is said to be descended from some of the aboriginal inhabitants of the country who were set to this work by the Aryan invaders. Though he is said to have been known originally by the name of Prajápti Pándey (equal to the great progenitor Brahman) and is sometimes addressed as Prajápati, Lord of creation, yet the Kumhár is universally despised and his trade looked down upon—a fact which is variously attributed to the poor character of the articles he manufactures, his

1

willingness to carry manure and sweepings and his hereditary association with that impure beast the donkey. Yet in spite of the poor esteem in which he is held, his aid is required at the two most important ceremonies of the Hindu religion, the marriage and the funeral. The bride must go to the Kumhárin to ward off the chance of being left a widow. She is seated on the wheel which is turned round seven times, and she and the Kumhárin exchange " páns " which both have touched with their lips. At a funeral the Kumhár must supply 13 " ghats," and must also replace the broken earthenware.

In some parts there are said to be as many as twelve sub-divisions in the caste, but the principal seem to be—

    (1)   The Bardia or bullock-driver.
    (2)   The Gadhaira or donkey driver.

So named from the animals which they employ to carry their goods to market. The social status of the former is the higher of the two, and a Brahman may take water from his hands, but the touch of the Gadhaira defiles. In Damoh the caste is divided into (i) Bardia and (ii) Sungaria (keeper of pigs).

The Kumhár is to be found in almost every village in the province. There were at the same time of the census report of 1891 102,682 Kumhárs in the province, forming 8 per cent. of the population. In Saugar and Damoh and the districts of the Narbuda valley they form as much as 1 per cent. of the population.

Materials.

Clay. The potter is not particular as to the clay he uses, and does not go far afield to seek for finer qualities but digs it from the nearest place in the neighbourhood, where he can obtain it free of cost. Clay is spoken of generally as of two kinds—(1) the red, (2) the black or káli mitti. The Seoni report says that red clay is obtained in the more hilly parts near the base of hills or on the higher elevations, generally intermixed with sand or murrum. The kali mitti, on the other hand, is obtained near towns in the beds of tanks, nálas, rivers or streamlets, and generally in places which are for a certain portion of the year under water. For red clay the potter has simply to dig one or two feet below the surface, and as his needs extend he draws upon the same shallow excavation for more.

Red clay is light and easy to manipulate, and is readily worked into a smooth surface. It is very generally used for making chillums, hookas and gamlas. Káli mitti is more ductile and tenacious, and is used in making vessels which are required for hard use.

The clay requires a good deal of preparation before it is ready for use. Stones and grit have first to be removed. To effect this the clay is well pounded and then thrown into a vessel full of water. The stones and grit sink to the bottom and then are removed by hand. The pure clay then gradually settles to the bottom, and after some three hours the surface water is drawn off and the clay is thrown upon a hard surface covered with ashes to dry. When the greater part of the moisture has been drawn off, the clay is ready for the purpose of kneading. At this stage other materials are added to the clay. In Saugor it appears to be the practice to mix the clay with an almost equal quantity of horse dung, varying according to the quality of the clay. Ashes are also added to prevent breakage during the process of baking, and for some vessels salt and saltpetre are added to increase their porousness and consequent cooling properties. The preparation is then put aside for a day or two to dry, after which it is ready for use.

At Messrs. Burns and Co.'s works in Jubbulpore, where the potter's branch of the business is said to be still in its infancy, a somewhat more elaborate process of preparation is employed. The clay is first ground in a regular machine made for the purpose, after which it is thrown into a vat, where it is left to the action of the water for one day. The whole contents of the vat are then passed into a vat on a lower level through a sieve which eliminates the stones and grit. After two days the second vat is opened and the clay is run out upon a long floor, when it is allowed to dry for two days. It is then collected in lumps and is ready for use.

Some of the larger vessels are made by hand alone, but the majority of articles of pottery are moulded upon the revolving wheel or "chák." The wheel.

This chák is either—

(i) a circular disc cut out of a single piece of stone about a yard in diameter or

(ii) an ordinary wooden wheel with two spokes forming two diameters at right angles. The rim is thickened by the addition of a coating of mud strengthened with fibre.

The wheel is supported on a small perpendicular iron pivot, which is fixed in the ground and fits into a hole in the centre of the lower surface of the wheel. When the wheel is of wood, a small round piece of stone is let into the hole which receives the pivot in order to prevent the wood wearing away. A slanting hole is made in the upper surface of the wheel near the rim to receive the stick "Chakrait" by which the wheel is turned.

The other instruments required by the potter are:—Thápa, a wooden mallet, used for beating vessels into shape while still moist, known in the Nagpur Division by the name of "Pitni."

" Suriya," or " Pindí," a stone about a seer in weight, flat on one side and convex on the other. The convex side is held against the inside of the vessel so as to support the blows of the mallet, known in the Nagpur Division by the name of " Gota " or " Dagad."

" Dora " or " Chhin, " a string for separating the moulded vessel from the rest of the clay.

" Patyámati" or " pota," a piece of cloth for smoothing the surface of the mould while it is on the wheel.

Kond, known in Nagpur as Potní, an open-mouthed clay pot filled with ashes and with a cloth stretched across the mouth, used as a rest upon which to beat out the mould.

" Chakora, " a dish full of water in which the potter constantly moistens his hands.

" Thapia, " a scraper used for sharpening the edges of the pots, known in Nagpur as " Chilni, " " Wacha " or " Saira. "

Other instruments in use in the Nagpur Division are Thasser, a small circular mould with points for producing marks upon the vessel.

" Cháp, " a stamp with different impressions for stamping the vessels before they are baked.

" Soogrim, " an instrument shaped like the end of a spur for stamping vessels.

" Sánchá, " or moulds, are also used in the manufacture of toys and bricks.

Method of manufacture. The method of manufacture seems to be much the same all over the Province. The following description is taken from the Saugor report :—

" When the clay is thoroughly kneaded and ready for use, a lump of it is placed on the centre of the wheel. The potter seats himself in front of the wheel, and fits his stick (Chakrait) into the slanting hole in the upper surface of the wheel. With this stick the wheel is made to revolve very rapidly and sufficient impetus is given to it to keep it in motion for several minutes. The potter then lays aside the stick, and with his hands moulds the lump of clay into the shape required, stopping every now and then and again to give the wheel a fresh spin as it loses its momentum. When satisfied with the shape of his vessel he separates it from the lump with the " Chhin " or piece of string mentioned above, and places it on a bed of ashes to prevent its sticking to the ground. Enough clay is always placed on the wheel for a considerable number of pots, so that a dozen or more are turned out without allowing the wheel to stop spinning."

Small vessels such as the " Dabla," " Dia, " " Bót," &c.. are finished on the wheel.

For the larger vessels a thick mould is first prepared on the wheel. This is allowed to dry slightly till the clay is tenacious enough to bear the blow of the " Thápa." It is then placed on the " Kond " and beaten out with the " Thápa," the " Pindí" being pressed against the inner surface as a support.

A few ashes are sprinkled over the mould, inside and out to prevent the " Thápa, " and Pindí from sticking to the moist clay. This beating is repeated till the required shape is attained. All cracks are then filled up with a mixture of sand and clay, and the vessel is put on one side to dry before baking. The smaller pots, while still slightly moist, are rubbed with shells to remove all inequalities.

No great advance appears to have been made upon these simple methods at Messrs. Burn and Co.'s works at Jubbulpore.

The sole improvement appears to be that the Chák is made to revolve by means of a hand-wheel connected with the Chák by a leathern strap or band.

The colouring and ornamentation are both of a very simple character, and the methods employed seem to be much the same in every district. The following description is taken from the Saugor report :—

" Before baking the pottery has to be coloured. Gairu or red ochre is used to give it a red and chalk to give it a white tinge. Black is obtained by putting goats' or sheep's dung in the kiln and completely stopping all outlets. The ware is impregnated by the smoke and turns a dull black.

The ornamentation is usually very primitive, consisting of some fairly simple design of circles and straight lines. The circles are made while the vessel is on the wheel. Cross marks are made afterwards by the " Kumhár " women with their nails. Black marks on a red or white ground are obtained by means of small nodules of black stone found in the beds of rivers and nalas. These the Kumhárs call " Mitti-ka-urda " from their resemblance in shape to the " Urda " bean.

Red marks on a white ground and white on red are obtained in a similar manner, but the secret of making red or white marks on a black ground has yet to be discovered. All these colours are "pakka" and are put on before baking. A brilliant sheen with a golden or silver tinge is imparted to chillams, toys and other small articles by means of a kind of imported clay probably impregnated with mica. When the ware is once baked the Kumhár will do nothing more to it. Any further ornamentation is done by the mochi, who paints various designs in colours, but the vessels painted by him are of no use except to send presents in.''

In the Bhandára District a coating of yellow clay is put on the vessels previous to baking in order to give them a glaze. This yellow mud is first soaked in water for 8 days and then strained and thickened by boiling. At Kaniwárá, in the Seoni District, a decoction is made from the bark of a tree called "tinsa," and the application of this is said to give a gloss to the vessel.

Potter's
kiln (bhatti
or awá). The potter's kiln (bhatti or awá) is of the simplest description. It is merely a deep hole in the ground in which the vessels to be baked and fuel are placed in alternate layers. The fuel used generally consists of cow-dung cakes (kandá), refuse grass and sweepings of all sorts, as fire-wood is too expensive. When all the vessels are arranged, a heap of rubbish is piled upon top, a central flue (nár) being left to create a draught and fire is applied from below. The colour of the flame indicates the heat of the kiln. If the flame burns green or blue it shows that the heat is too intense and earth is thrown upon the kiln to cool it down. If the flame burns pale, then the fire is too slow and holes are made in the cover to increase the draught. A bright-red flame shows that the kiln is at a temperature which will bake the vessels thoroughly without burning or cracking them.' From 100 to 300 vessels are baked in a single bhatti, the number varying within these limits with the character of the vessels and the capacity of the kiln. The writer of the Seoni report says :—

"The length of time for baking differs according to the quality and colour of the vessels. Red vessels or ware take 3 hours, black 4 hours, and tiles take two nights. The kiln is allowed to burn for three hours when a small stone is thrown on the vessels, and, if the vessels give a ringing sound, the fire is extinguished and it is allowed to cool down till morning. Vessels are usually baked the night before the bazar-day in each village. Owing to the primitive character of the kiln, its capacity and the time required for baking are not uniform.''

The following description is given in the Jubbulpore report of the kilns used at Messrs. Burn and Co.'s works :—" Special kilns are constructed for baking articles of pottery. The ordinary kilns used for tiles and pipes are not suitable, as it is important that all smoke should be excluded and that the flames should not come into contact with the clay. The kilns used are known as "muffled kilns" and are covered at the top by a double roof. The flames from the furnaces play upon the lower side of the floors, and spread themselves upwards, working between the two roofs. By this means the pottery is entirely isolated from all con-

taminating influences, such as dust and smoke. The kilns are heated up
to a bright-red heat for 4 days, after which they are left to cool for 3 days
more. The pottery is then taken out and immersed in the glazing solu-
tion which is procured from England. After this the glaze is burnt into
the pottery by another five days' baking in the kiln. The article on being
taken from the kiln is ready for the market.

The following is a list of the principal articles manufactured in the
Province, which are chiefly vessels used for household purposes :—

"*Ghada,*" a vessel used for storing and cooling water, average *Water-pots. &c.*
price one pice, " Ghela," "Thilia," "Dabla" and "Dabliya" are all smaller
varieties of the same vessel, the price of which varies from four for one
pice to one pice each. A larger kind is the " Matka" used for storing
grain, &c., and also used for cooling water. To the same class belong
two vessels known as the " Koonda " and " Paina." The former is used
for storing flour and the latter for storing vegetables. Their price is
about 2 to 3 pies each.

Mahomedans are said to prefer metal pots to store their grain in, but
earthen-ware vessels are universally used for cooling water. If used for
cooking purposes by a Hindu family, a new ghada is used every day, as
the vessel is supposed to be tainted when it has been used for such a
purpose once. The cooling qualities of a "ghada" become impaired
after about a fortnight's use, but exposure to heat restores the porosity of
the vessel. If treated with care they will last for as long as two years
or more.

The "Suráhí," or "Kunjá" as it is also called in Sambalpore, is a
"ghada" with a long neck and sometimes handles. It is commonly
used by all classes of Natives and also by Europeans as a receptacle for
drinking water. It has all the cooling properties of the "ghada."

Piyálá a cup for drinking water. "Parayá" a dish for food. *Vessels for cooking, eating, drinking, &c.*
" Kathorá" another kind of cup. "Kallá " or " Taiyá" and " Tawá" are
dishes used for making roti. " Handí," for cooking rice, &c. " Dohní"
a vessel used as a milking pail.

These vessels are used chiefly by Mahomedans and Hindus of lower
castes. Brahmans and other high caste Hindus prefer to use metal
vessels.

The same vessels as are used for storing water are also used to store *Vessels used for the storage of grain, &c.*
grain and similar articles. Amongst these are the "Kanhári." "Matká,"
"Nánd" and "Dablá." A Kanhari costs annas 2, a matka anna 1, a
Nand annas 1½ or annas 2 and a Dabla one pice.

The "Dablá" is also used for keeping ghee and oil, but metal vessels
are preferred by those able to afford them. "Chapiá" or "Parchhiá "
are smaller varieties of the same vessel.

Vessels used for agricultural purposes. " Bót " is a small vessel with a narrow mouth used to keep oil in. The " Ghariá " or " Kahentá " is a small pot attached to the rope of a Persian wheel to raise water for irrigation purposes. The price is about annas 8 per 100.

" Nánds " are used by syces to store water for their horses, by cattle-owners as feeding and drinking troughs, and by masons to keep the water required for their work.

Pipes, &c. " Huqqas " and various kinds of " chillams " for smoking both tobacco and ganja are manufactured in every district.

" Kundiás " or " gamlás " are used and shaped like the ordinary English flower-pot.

Lamps, &c. " Diá " or " chirág " is the commonest kind of lamp used by the poorer classes. It is a plain open saucer in which a wick is placed floating in the oil. The oil used is of country manufacture. At the Dewáli festival the very poorest people purchase some of these lamps to illuminate their houses. Price anna one per 100. " Dabbí " is a lamp used for burning kerosine oil. It is merely a round pot with a narrow opening in which a pipe containing the wick is placed. Price, 2 pice.

" Gwálin " or cowherd woman.—This is a small figure of a woman supporting a number of tiny . saucers each of which is in fact a smaller edition of the " dia " described above. It is used for illuminations in the " Dewáli " festival at which time there is a great demand for this article. Its price varies from two pice to an anna.

Sénkí, a saucer in which incense is burnt, price one pice.

Toys. Earthenware toys seem to be manufactured in most districts. An idea of their merit may be obtained from the following extract from a district Report :—" Toys deserve more than a passing mention, some few are turned on the wheel, but the greater part are made by hand. Some advance has certainly been made of late years in their finish, but there is yet much to be desired. They usually represent animal or human figures without, of course, any idea of anatomical proportion. At the same time it is never hard to tell what any particular figure is meant to represent, if not from direct resemblance, at least from some characteristic mark.

A quadruped with yellow stripes will probably be a tiger, one with spiral horns a black buck, and a biped, when crowned with a very large topi, a 'Sáhib' or ' Gorú Ádmi.' The very grotesqueness and absurd shapes of these articles, have however, with their gaudy colouring, a peculiar charm of their own. At the same time some representations of deities of the Hindu Pantheon, made and coloured by a few of the better trained workmen of Saugor, are really beautiful. The toy trade is confined almost entirely to the city of Saugor. The demand for toys is considerable but spasmodic, arising as it does only during melas and festivals. The opportunities offered by this branch of the industry have been seized almost entirely by the mochi to the exclusion of Kumhar." In the Nagpur district, the images made by Kumhars, are said to fetch sometimes as high a price as Rs. 25.

The following articles are manufactured at Messrs. Burn & Co's. Works, Jubalpur:—Jam pots, filters, vases, battery jars, porous cells, closet pans, Commissariat articles, spittoons, cream dishes, &c. *Miscellaneous.*

The Kumhár seems to be anything but a prosperous member of the community. From every district comes the same account that he lives from hand to mouth and can, with difficulty, make both ends meet. He is additionally handicapped by the fact that during the rains his work is at a stand-still, so that he has to make enough during 8 months to support him for the whole year. His profits are variously estimated at from, annas 2 to annas 4 per diem, but the writer of the Bhandára report says, that in a personally investigated case, he found that the profits on the whole work done by a potter, his wife and his daughter, during 8 days, amounted to Rs. 2-4 only. The writer of the Seoni report says :— *Earnings of Potter.*

" The Kumhár or potter gets one sheaf of rice or wheat from every " field as his due in a malguzari village on condition of his supplying " vessels free of cost to the cultivators, but he charges non-cultivators " the market price, which varies according to the size of the vessel. The " average earnings of a potter's family is from 2 to 4 annas a day, for the " whole family. They live generally from hand to mouth and are " steeped in debt. If the family of a potter is large, some members of " the family take to cultivation, and, if by good luck, any succeeds in " saving money, he becomes the village banker. But the potter agricul- " turist, like other cultivators, is generally steeped in debt."

The condition of the Kumhár seems to be somewhat more prosperous in Sambalpur where his earnings are estimated at, from Rs. 8 to Rs. 20 a month.

No export or import trade in pottery exists in the province. The villagers are generally content to buy their pots from their own village potter, though it sometimes happens that the ware of some particular place will obtain a district celebrity, as in Saugor, where the Shahgarh pottery is much sought after. The superiority of the ware is due to the quality of the clay found at Shahgarh, and not to any difference in the workmanship. *Trade.*

There seems to be no ground for hoping that the industry will improve and the prospect seems to be rather the reverse. No advance has *Prospects of the Industry.*

3

been made in the methods of manufacture and the demand seem to be falling off. Metal vessels and cheap European China have replaced pottery to a large extent, and the universal kerosene tin is now used, everywhere for such purposes as boiling water, &c. A certain demand however, must always continue, as the rough country-made pottery is, owing to its cooling qualities, incomparable as a receptacle for storing water.

GLASS.

The principal article of glass ware, produced in the province, is the ordinary glass bangle worn by every native woman.

Caste of glass-workers. Both Hindus and Mahomedans engage in the trade, the former being known by the name of Kachaira and the latter by the names of Shishgár and Turkári. At the last census it was estimated that there were 1898 Kachairas, 574 Turkáris and 865 Shishgárs in the Province.

The material is no longer manufactured in the province, but is imported from the North-West Provinces.

Furnace. The method of preparing the glass is uniform throughout the province. The furnace is built partially underground and is covered with a dome containing 5 or 6 small apertures (ghariya). Inside each opening there is a bracket or ledge of earth to serve as a support upon which to rest the glass, that is being melted. Each "ghariya" is divided into two compartments, one for the glass and one for the colour. Small walls, about 2 inches thick and 6 inches high running out from the furnace, form a separate compartment in front of each opening. Each workman has a separate compartment. In front of each workman a stone slab is fixed, and in front of this again, is a sink. The firewood is kept over the furnace on a sort of canopy 3 or 4 feet high supported on wooden uprights. The wood is thus dried and is also within easy reach. At either end of the furnace is a large opening, the one for admitting the fuel, and the other for regulating the draught.

The instruments used in glass-making are—" Ánkri " an iron rod about 2½ to 3 feet long with a hook at the end.

" Patá, " a broad but tapering instrument about 7 to 9 inches long, used for pressing the glass.

" Salak " or " Sarang " an iron bar about 2 feet long. " Khootla " an instrument to give size and shape to the bangles. It is an iron bar with a cone of clay called " Kalbut" at the end.

" Palla " " Chamchi " or "Karchhila" a spoon for placing the glass inside the furnace to melt.

" Thapta " or " Badhaunis " a thin pointed bar of iron with a wooden handle.

Method of making churis. In the manufacture of bangles or "churis" the furnace is first heated and then ordinary glass, pounded up, is placed in one of the compartments of the ledge ("Gharia") and coloured glass is placed in the other. The glass is tested with the "Sarang," and when it is melted into a thick viscous fluid, it is raised on the hook of the "Ankri" and fixed on the point of the "Sarang." It is then taken out of the furnace on the point of the "Sarang" and turned on the stone slab with the left hand and patted gently with the "Pata" to form the mass into a ring of equal thickness. The mass, still on the point of the "Sarang", is again put on the ledge in the furnace and gently turned round and round while the coloured glass from the other compartment is dropped on it by means of the "Badhaunia." The "Sarang" is again taken out and the colouring is made even by turning the glass on the slab and patting it with the patta. The ring is then detached with a gentle stroke. It is then again heated and twisted round and round on the point of the "Badhaunia" to make it larger and thinner. It is then further extended by being placed on the "Kalbut," which is rested on the stone slab and twisted round. When the required size is obtained, the "Churi" is slipped off the "Kalbut" into the sink.

The imported glass is plain and is coloured locally. The Saugor report contains the most detailed account of the various colours produced, and the method of colouring.

Colouring.

Green (Hará). One seer of glass is heated with half a chiták of copper reduced to ashes. A little salt is sometimes added and often brass filings are substituted for copper.

Yellow (Pílá). Five parts of lead and one of pewter are reduced to powder. This mixture is heated with four to six times its bulk of glass.

Red (Lál). Pewter, lead and zinc in the proportion of $6:5:1$ are reduced to ashes and heated with four or five times the quantity of glass.

Black (Kálá). Eight parts of glass heated with one of powdered iron.

Blue (Baigni). This colour is obtained by means of a stone called shend imported from the Rámtek Tahsil of the Nagpur District. This shend is powered and mixed with four times the quantity of glass.

Indigo (Nílá). An iron dross coloured metalloid, is imported from Nepal. This costs about Rs. 4 a seer. It is mixed with glass in the proportion of $1:16$. This colour is a very favourite one.

Purple brown (Udá). A particular kind of soft stone, is brought from Tiki Toria, a hillock near Rehli. It is reduced to powder by friction, and two "chitáks" of the powder are mixed with three seers of glass and half a "chiták" of "saféd hataiya," a white nodular stone in powder. Light green (Jangáli) is obtained by mixing a little yellow with the green (hará) described above.

Preferences for cértain colours seem to exist among the various classes of the people. The Hindus prefer black and indigo. Blue and yellow are admissible, but green (hará or jangáli) is never worn. The Musalmans keep, as a rule, to light green and black. The other colours are admissible, but not often worn.

Varieties and ornamentation of Churis. Churis are generally named simply according to their colours. Some varieties, however, have specific names, e.g.—

"Bangalia," flat, with raised edges forming a grove, ornamented with red and yellow stripes.

"Kará," round, with yellow cross lines on a red ground.

"Munaiyan," a green ground with yellow cross lines.

"Dorangá," or parti-coloured half red and half yellow.

"Maithí," red with small yellow dots, named after the yellow seed of the Fenugreek.

"Dhar," very thin with a sharp edge, this may be of any colour.

"Khaggá," flat and usually coloured black. The "Khaggá" is worn by low caste women on the arm above the elbow joint.

There are also other varieties too numerous to describe, such as "Chakiá," "Dochallá," "Soráhi," "Kachmirá," "Putlí," "Gullá," "Pakiá," "Ánkrá," "Kaisar," &c. The method of ornamenting bangalias is as follows :—Pieces of red and yellow glass are drawn into thin wires with the "Ankri." These are spun together while hot, and then allowed to cool. This wire is then broken into small pieces which are affixed to the Churi, while it is still a small thick ring before being opened out.

Profits, &c. The average earnings of a "Churígár" are estimated at about annas 2 to 6 per diem. The cost of the raw material is about Rs. 8 per maund including cost of carriage. One seer of glass will yield about 200 churis, of which the average workman can turn out about 500 in a day. They are sold at 8 to 14 for a pice in the bazar. Deducting the cost of fuel and the profits of the middle man, the average earnings may be taken to be about annas 4. Both Hindu and Musalman women wear Churis. To the former they are indispensable during the lifetime

of their husbands. On the death of her husband a Hindu woman breaks
her glass bangles and substitutes metal ones. Amongst the lower
castes, where widows are allowed to remarry, the first ceremony is for
the bridegroom to place Churis on the wrists of the widow. The phrase
"Churi pahinana" has from this come to mean to marry a widow.

There appears to be practically no import or export trade in these *Trade,*
Churis. The majority of districts supply their own wants in this
respect, and though glass bangles of European manufacture are said to
be both cheaper and better made, they do not appear to command any
large sale.

The manufacture of glass-ware, other than Churis, is extremely *Other glass-*
limited. Rough globes used as pendants from ceilings, pen-holders, *ware.*
small flasks (Shíshís), jars for sacred water, the symbolic Mahádeo and
small mirrors are occasionally made, but only in very small quantities.

The articles turned out by the local Churígár are generally good *Prospects of*
enough to satisfy the wants of his customers, but were the trade in *the trade,*
European glass pushed, the industry would probably die out. The great
obstacle to any revival in the industry is the cost of firewood, of which
a large quantity is required. The primitive and faulty construction of
the furnaces too would prevent work of any merit being turned out.
If cheap fuel were obtainable and larger furnaces could be erected and
maintained under skilled superintendence, it is possible that good results
might be obtained. It is doubtful, however, if any such project is worth
undertaking.

The total number of glass-workers in the province is very small
and their life is very unhealthy. The heat and glare to which they are
exposed undermines the constitution and ruins the eyesight of those
engaged in the trade. There is in fact a Hindí saying to the effect that
"when a Kachaira bears a son, the turner rejoices, for it is certain that
premature blindness will overtake him and send him perforce to the
turner to pull the straps of his lathe."

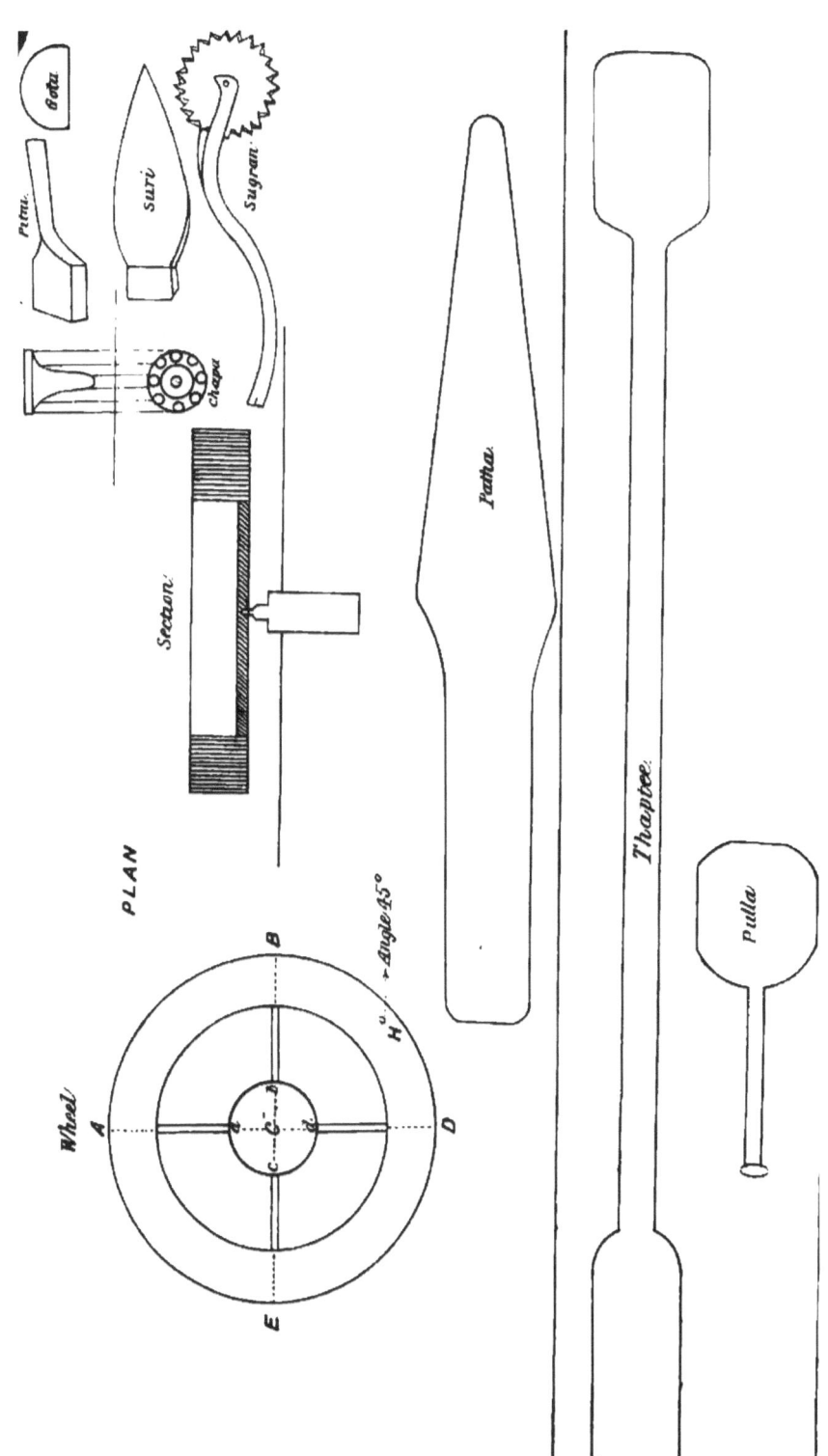

Pem.

Gota.

Sulti.

Sugran.

Chapa

Section.

PLAN

Wheel

Patha.

Thaptee.

Pulla

B

A

D

E

H

Angle 45°

C

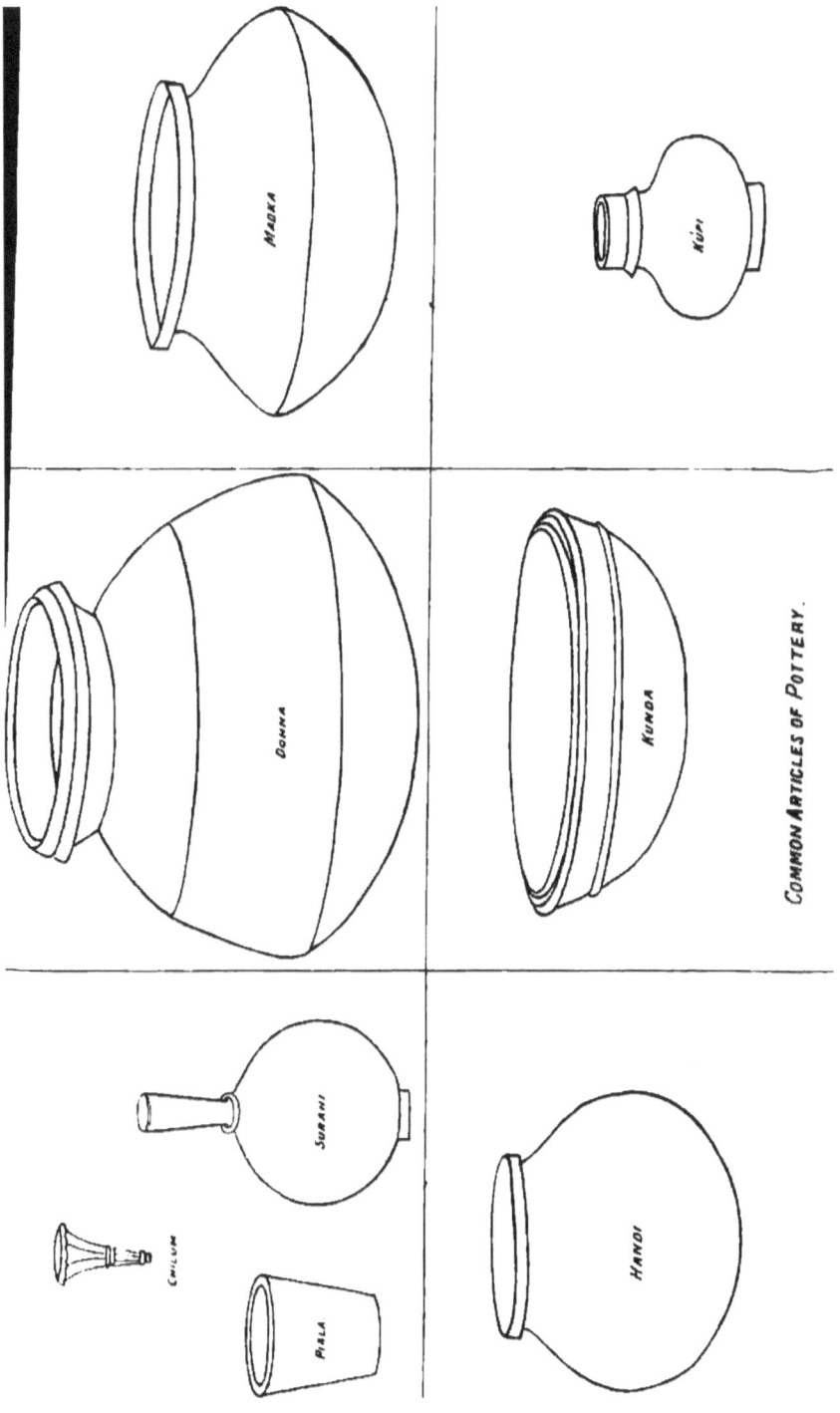

COMMON ARTICLES OF POTTERY.

GWALIN ANOTHER FASHION.

GWALIN or CLAY WORSHIPPED IN DEWALI.

Glass Instruments

Saargayna.   I

Suaring   III

Chamchi   VII

Badhanna.   V

Ankali   II

Patka   IV

Kalbit   VI